Aesop did not write down his fables. He told many people the stories and they remembered them. It was nearly two hundred years later before all the stories were collected together and published.

The fables were not published in English until the fifteenth century, but since then they have been read by people all over the world. Their moral lessons are as true today as they were 2,500 years ago when Aesop was alive.

Contents

First edition

© LADYBIRD BOOKS LTD   MCMLXXXIII

0 7214 7523 X

Aesop's Fables

retold by
Marie Stuart and
Audrey Daly

with illustrations by
Robert Ayton

Ladybird Books Loughborough

The dog and his reflection

One day, a dog took a bone from a shop.
He ran off with it before anyone could catch him.

He came to a river and went over the bridge. As he looked
down into the water, he saw another dog with a bone! He
did not know that the dog he saw in the water was a
reflection of himself.

"That dog has a big bone. It is as big as mine," he said.
"I will jump into the water and take it from him."

So in he jumped.

When he was in the water, he could not see the other dog,
and he could not see the other bone either.

He had lost his own bone, too, because it fell as he jumped in.

So, because he was greedy, he got nothing in the end.

Moral:

*If you want more because you are greedy, in
the end you might find you have less.*

The fox without a tail

One day a fox ran into a trap. He pulled and pulled to get away from it. At last he did, but his tail came off. It was left in the trap.

He did not like the way he looked without a tail.
"All the other foxes will make fun of me," he said.
"What can I do?
I know, I will make them think it is better not to have a tail."

So he said to the other foxes,
"You would look better without tails. What use are they anyway? Look at me. I can run very fast because I have no tail."

But one old fox said,
"You say that, only because you have lost your own tail. That is why you do not want us to have tails. We like our tails, and we shall keep them, thank you."

Moral:

Wise people are not easily fooled.

4

The shepherd boy and the wolf

Once there was a boy who lived on a farm. Every day he had to take his father's sheep to a hill a long way off. He did not like being there on his own.

One day, he said to himself,
"I will call Wolf! Wolf!
Then everyone will think that a wolf has come to eat my sheep.

People will run to help me. It will be fun when they find out there is no wolf after all."

So he did call "Wolf! Wolf!" and everyone ran to help him.

When they came he did not thank them. He just said,
"There is no wolf. It was only a joke. Now you will all have to go back home again."

He did this three times. Each time he told them that there was no wolf.

Then one day the wolf **did** come.
"Help! help! The wolf is here!" called the boy.

But everyone said,
"We know that there is no wolf. He just calls us for fun. There is no danger. This time we will not go."

So they did not go and the wolf killed all the sheep.

Moral:

If we tell lies, no one will believe us when we speak the truth.

6

The fir tree and the bramble

One day, on a hill top, a fir tree said to a bramble bush, "Look at me, I am tall, strong, graceful and very beautiful. What good are you? You are small, ugly and untidy."

This made the bramble bush very unhappy because it knew the fir tree was right.

But next day some men carrying axes came up the hill.

They started to chop down the fir tree. They wanted to use it to make a new house.

"Oh dear!" cried the fir tree, as it started to fall. "I wish I were a bramble bush, then the men would not have cut me down."

Moral:

People who are too proud may be sorry later.

The boastful traveller

A man once went to a place he had never been to before. It was a long way off and he was there for a year. When he went home, he wanted to talk about it all the time.

Everyone said,
"Why is he always telling us about that place? We don't want to know about it."

They asked him, "Why did you come back if it was so nice?"
"I came back to tell you about it," said the man, and he went on talking.

"In that place," he said,
"all the men can jump well.

One day we wanted to see who could jump the best. So we all had a try. My jump was the best. I am a very good jumper. If you had been there at the time, you would have seen how good I am."

"We do not have to go all that way to see you jump," said one of the men.
"You can let us see how well you can do it here. So jump **now**!"

Moral:

People who boast are soon found out.

The ant and the dove

One hot day, an ant went to the river to get a drink of water. But he fell in and could not get out.

A dove saw that the ant was in danger.
"I must help him," she said.
"If I pick up this leaf and drop it in the water, the ant can get on it. It will be like a little boat."

So the dove dropped a leaf in the water and the ant climbed onto it.

"Thank you, Mrs Dove," called the ant.
"I will help you one day."

Soon after, a man came along with a bow and arrow. He saw the dove on the tree and was going to shoot at her.

Just then the ant came along and bit the man on the leg.

This made the man jump and his arrow went up into the sky. The arrow missed the dove, so she flew away out of danger.

"Thank you, little ant," cooed the dove.
"You did help me after all."

Moral:

No one is too little to be helpful.

The crow and the fox

One day a big, black crow found some cheese.

"I will fly up into this tree with it," she said.
"I want to eat it now."

A fox came by and saw the bird. He saw the cheese as well.
He, too, wanted to eat the cheese.

He went round and round the tree while he thought how
he could get the cheese.

Then he said to the crow,
"You look very nice.
If you can sing very nicely as well, I think you must be
Queen of all the birds."

The crow was very pleased. She liked to be called a Queen.
"Yes, I can sing," she said.

But as she said this the cheese fell from her beak.

Down to the ground it fell. The fox picked up the cheese
and ran away.

"You may be Queen of the birds. You may look nice and
you may sing well. But you do not think very well," he
said, as he ran off.

Moral:

*Beware of people who say nice things they do
not mean.*

The boys and the frogs

One day, four boys went out to play near a pond.

Some frogs lived in the pond. It was their home.

One bad boy saw the frogs and said to the other boys,
"Come on! Let's make them jump out of the water.
It will be fun!"

So they all looked for something to throw at the frogs.

A little frog saw what they were doing.

He did not like what he saw.

So he hopped onto a floating leaf in front of the boys.
"STOP!" shouted the little frog.
"You would not like to have stones thrown at you if you
were frogs. It may be fun for you, but it is no fun for us!"

Moral:

*Do not do things to other people that you
would not like done to you.*

Who will bell the cat?

Once some mice lived in a house.

A big cat lived in the house too.

Every day she liked to eat some of the mice.

At last they said to one another,
"This must stop, or soon we shall all be eaten. Let us all think what we can do."

After a time an old mouse said,
"I know what we can do. One of us must put a bell on the cat.

The bell will tell us when she is near and when we must stay at home. After she has gone away, we can come out again."

"Yes. That will be a wise thing to do. Let us do that," they all said.

"But which one of us will put the bell on her?" said the old mouse. "I am too old, I cannot run very fast so I don't think I can do it."

"So are we," said some of the others.

"And we are too little," said the baby mice.

In the end no one would do it.

So the bell was never put on the cat and she went on eating the mice.

Moral:

Some things are more easily said than done.

The raven and the jug

A big, black raven wanted a drink.

She saw a big jug with water at the bottom.

She could not reach the water and wondered what to do.

"I know," she said.
"I shall put some stones in the jug. Then the water will come up to the top."

After the first stone, the water rose a little. Then she put in another stone, and the water rose more.

She put more and more stones in until the water came up to the top of the jug.

"Now I can reach the water. At last I can have a drink," said the raven.

So she had a very long drink.

Moral:

If you try hard enough, you may find you can do something that at first seems very difficult.

The dog in the manger

One day a dog ran into a stable and jumped into the manger.

The manger had some hay in it.

When the horse and cow wanted to eat their hay, the dog would not let them.

"You don't eat hay, so you don't need it," said the cow.

"We want the hay. It is ours. It is our dinner," said the horse.

But the dog said, "If I can't eat it, then I shall not let you eat it either!"

"Why?" asked the cow.

"Why?" asked the horse.

"Because I don't like to see you eat what I can't eat too," said the dog. "Go away!"

So the horse and the cow had to go away hungry.

Moral:

Do not stop others having what you don't need.

The lion and the hare

Once a lion found a hare. He was just going to eat her when a stag ran by.

"That stag will make me a bigger dinner," he said.

So he let the hare go and ran after the stag. But the stag could run very, very fast and soon it got right away.

When the lion saw that he could not catch the stag, he said, "I will go back for the hare."

But when he came to the place where the hare had been, he found that she had gone.

"I should have had her for my dinner when I first saw her," said the lion.
"I wanted too much and now I have nothing."

Moral:

It is sometimes wiser to be content with what you have.

The fox and the grapes

A fox saw some nice grapes.

"They look good," he said.
"I want to eat them, but they are too high for me. I must try jumping for them." He jumped and jumped.

Again and again he jumped but he could not reach the grapes.

So he said, "I can see now that they are green. They are not sweet. I do not like green grapes. They are sour. I don't want them."

So he went away without any.

He knew that the grapes were really very nice. He just said they were sour because he could not reach them.

Moral:

It is silly to say that you do not want something just because you cannot have it.

The crow and the swan

A crow once saw a swan and said to her,
"How nice you look! I wish I were white like you. I do not like being black."

He saw that the swan was always in the water.

"If I get in the water, I may become white too," he said.

So he got into the water, but he was still black when he came out.

"Let me think," he said.
"If I **stay** in the water that may make me white."

Before the crow went into the water, he could fly about to look for food. He always found something to eat.

He did not like fish and could find nothing else to eat in the water.

So he did not live very long, nor did he become white.

Moral:

Think well before you copy other people.

Brother and sister

Once there was a man who had two children, a boy and a girl. The boy was good looking, but the girl was not.

One day they found a mirror and for the first time, saw what they looked like. The boy was very pleased.

He said to his sister, "How handsome I am! I look much nicer than you!"

The girl did not like what he said and gave her brother a push.
"Go away!" she said.

Their father saw what was happening and said to the boy, "You must always **be** good as well as **look** good."

And to the girl he said,
"My dear, if you help everyone and do your best to please, everyone will love you. It will not matter that you are not as good looking as your brother."

Moral:

*It is better to **be** good than to be just good looking.*

30

The fox and the lion

One day a fox saw a lion.

It was the first time he had ever seen one.

The lion looked so big that the fox did not know what to do. He ran away as fast as he possibly could.

Soon he saw the lion again.

This time the fox said,
"I saw you the other day. I don't like the look of you.
You are too big. You might want to eat me."

And he ran away again.

As he ran, he said to himself,
"The lion did not eat me last time."

So this time he did not run so fast.

Next day he saw the lion again and did not run away at all.

"Good morning, Mr Lion," he said.
"I have seen you before. You do not look so big today. I am not afraid of you any more."

So he sat down to have a long chat with the lion.

Moral:

Things are not always what they seem to be at first.

The goose that laid the golden eggs

Once an old man and an old woman had a goose. Their goose was not like other geese because its eggs were different. They were made of gold.

Every day the goose laid a golden egg for the old man and the old woman.

They sold the eggs for a lot of money. But the more money they had the more they wanted.

They said, "If our goose lays golden eggs she must be made of gold. So let us cut her open and get out all the gold at once. Then we will have more money."

So they killed the goose, but found no gold.

When their goose was cut open they saw that she was just like any other goose.

And after that there were no more golden eggs. So they did not get any more money. They had nothing left in the end.

Moral:

A greedy man can lose all he has.

The bear and the travellers

One day, two men were on a journey when they saw a bear.

At first, the bear did not see them.

One man got up into a tree as fast as he could.

The other man was slow.
"Please help me up," he called.

But the first man went further up the tree and left him on his own.

"What can I do?" said the man under the tree.
"If I run away, the bear will see me. If he sees me, he will eat me."

So he lay on the ground and did not move.

The bear came up and walked all around him.

At last it went away.

The man in the tree came down.

He said, "The bear came very close to you. Did he say anything?"

"Yes," said the other man.
"The bear said, 'Never go for a walk with a man who leaves you when you are in danger.'"

Moral:

A real friend will not leave you to face trouble alone.

The wind and the sun

One day the wind said to the sun,
"Look at that man walking along the road. I can get his cloak off more quickly than you can."

"We will see about that," said the sun.
"I will let you try first."

So the wind tried to make the man take off his cloak. He blew and blew, but the man only pulled his cloak more closely around himself.

"I give up," said the wind at last.
"I cannot get his cloak off."

Then the sun tried. He shone as hard as he could. The man soon became hot and took off his cloak.

"I have won," said the sun.
"I made him take his cloak off."

Moral:

Kindness often gets things done more quickly than force.

38

The fox and the stork

One day, a fox said to a stork,
"Would you like to come to my house for dinner?"

"Yes, please," said the stork.
"That will be very nice."

But when the stork reached the fox's house, he found that the fox had put the dinner on two flat plates.

The stork could not eat anything because of his long beak.

The fox soon ate his own dinner and then said to the stork, "Don't you like your dinner? If you cannot eat any of it then I will eat it for you."

So he had his own dinner and the stork's dinner as well.

Soon after, the stork asked the fox to dinner.

The stork put the food in two jugs which had long necks.

This time it was the fox who could not reach the food.

He had to watch while the stork ate both dinners.

Moral:

If you play mean tricks on other people, they might do the same to you.

The trees and the axe

Once a man wanted to cut down some trees to make a house, but he could not use his axe because it had no handle.

So he went to the top of a hill where there were many trees and said to them,
"May I take a tree from this hill?"

But he did not tell them why.

The trees said to one another,
"Let us give him a very little tree. Then he will go away and not ask us for anything more."

So they gave him a little tree and the man went home.

When he got there he made a handle for his axe.

Then he went back to the hill and began to cut down the other trees.

"If we had not let him have the little tree he could not have cut us down," they said.

But it was too late.

The trees were all cut down.

Moral:

Be careful when you give way over small things, or you may have to give way over big ones.

The man and the partridge

One day, a fat partridge who was very hungry wandered into a bird trap.

She gobbled up the food that was in the trap and then found that she could not get out.

The man who had set the trap arrived soon after.

He was very pleased to see such a plump bird in his trap.

The partridge was very unhappy and begged him to let her go.

"Oh please, good sir," she pleaded, "if you will set me free, I will lead all my friends into your trap. Then you will have many more birds to eat."

The man took the plump partridge from his trap and said, "If you would do that, then you surely deserve to die. You are a wicked bird to want to do such a shameful thing."

Having said this, he took the partridge home for his supper.

Moral:

No one loves a traitor.

The eagle and the snake

An eagle was flying slowly along, looking for something to eat, when he saw a big snake lying in the sunshine.

He swooped down and seized it, but the snake was too quick for him. It wrapped its coils round him in a moment, and they began to fight.

A farmer working nearby heard the noise of the struggle, and came to see what was happening.

He helped the eagle to get free, but the snake was angry with him. It spat some of its poison into his drinking cup before gliding away. Luckily the eagle saw the snake take its revenge. As soon as the farmer lifted his cup to drink, the eagle knocked it out of his hand. The contents spilled on the ground, and the farmer was safe.

Moral:

One good turn deserves another.

The hare and the tortoise

The hare was always making fun of the tortoise because he was so slow on his feet.

After a while, the tortoise grew very tired of this.

One day, when the hare started to tease him again, he said, "You're not as quick as you think you are. Let's have a race — I bet I'll win!"

The hare began to laugh.
"All right, then," he said, "let's try and see. We'll have to find someone to judge the race, and set a course for us."

So they asked the fox, and he set a course for them and agreed to be the judge.

When the three met on the morning of the race, the hare could hardly speak for laughing, he thought the idea of the tortoise beating him was so funny.

At last came the time for the race. The two animals started off together, but the hare was soon so far ahead that he thought he might as well have a rest. He lay down — and fell fast asleep.

Meanwhile the tortoise plodded on. He saw the hare sleeping, but passed by without waking him.

At last the hare woke up, and dashed on at his fastest — but the tortoise had already won the race.

Moral:

Slow but steady can sometimes win the race.

The bull and the mouse

A bull which was very large and fierce was kept in a field with a wall all round.

One day, as he was grazing, he trod on a mouse's tail. The mouse was so cross that he bit the bull on the nose.

The bull chased him, but the mouse was too quick for him. He slipped into a hole in the wall, out of reach.

The bull charged furiously at the wall, again and again. At last he sank to the ground, tired out.

The mouse waited until all was quiet once more, then he darted out — and bit the bull again!

The bull started to his feet furiously — but by that time the mouse was back in his hole.

All the bull could do was to bellow in helpless anger. After a while, he heard a little voice say from inside the wall, "You see, you big fellows don't always have it all your own way. We little ones sometimes manage to get the best of it."

Moral:

The biggest and strongest doesn't always win.

The donkey and the pedlar

There was once a pedlar who travelled round the country with his donkey. He bought all sorts of things in the towns to sell to people in the villages. His donkey was always complaining that he had to carry too much.

One day the pedlar bought some salt to sell. He loaded up the baskets on the donkey with as much as he could carry.

On the way home, as they were crossing a stream, the donkey tripped and fell. The salt got wet, and disappeared into the water. When the donkey got to his feet, his load was much lighter.

The pedlar was very cross, and he drove the donkey back to town to buy more salt. When the baskets were full once more, they set out again.

As soon as they came to the stream, the donkey lay down in it. When he stood up, the salt had disappeared, just as before. The donkey was very pleased with himself, but the pedlar decided to teach him a lesson.

They went back to town yet again, and *this* time the pedlar filled the baskets with sponges. On the way home, the donkey, laughing to himself, lay down in the stream. But when he tried to stand up, he found that his load was now much heavier. Instead of disappearing as the salt had, the sponges had soaked up the water!

Moral:

The same trick never works twice.

The bat and the weasel

A young bat was flying around one evening when an owl suddenly flew out of a tree.

The owl's wing knocked the bat to the ground.
As he lay there, breathless, a weasel caught him.

He was about to be killed and eaten when he looked up at the weasel.
"Please let me go!" he pleaded.

"I can't do that," said the weasel. "I have to kill any birds that I find, because I am their enemy."

"But I'm *not* a bird," said the bat. "I'm a mouse."

The weasel looked down at him.
"So you are!" he said, and he let the little bat go.

Not long after this, the bat was caught again – and by another weasel.
"Please let me go," he asked, as before.

"No," said the weasel.
"I have to kill any mice that I find, because I am their enemy."

"But I'm *not* a mouse," said the little bat.
"Surely you can see I'm a bird!"

The weasel looked down at him. "So you are, now I come to look at you." And the bat went free once more!

Moral:

*Find out which way the wind is blowing
before you make up your mind.*

The lark and the farmer

A lark who was looking for a place to nest chose a field of corn.

Her eggs hatched, and the baby birds grew quickly under cover of the corn as it ripened.

Then one day, before the young larks could fly properly, the farmer came to look at the crop. It was yellowing, and he said,
"I will have to ask my neighbours to come and help me to reap this field."

One of the young larks heard him say this, and was very frightened. She went to her mother and said that the family should move house at once.

Her mother calmed her.
"There's no hurry," she said.
"A man who looks to his friends for help will take his time about a thing."

Then, a few days later, the farmer came to look at his crop again. By this time, the corn was so ripe that it was falling out of the ears on to the ground.

"I can put it off no longer," said the farmer.
"I will hire men and we'll start work at once."

The lark heard him. She said to her family,
"Come, we must be off. He isn't going to get his friends to help him this time, he is going to do the job himself."

Moral:

The best person to help you is yourself.